Trudy

Henry Cole

Greenwillow Books

An Imprint of HarperCollins*Publishers*

Trudy

Copyright © 2009 by Henry Cole

All rights reserved. Manufactured in China.

www.harpercollinschildrens.com

Acrylic paints were used to prepare the full-color art.

The text type is 16-point Berling Roman.

Library of Congress Cataloging-in-Publication Data

Cole, Henry, (date).

Trudy / by Henry Cole.

p. cm.

"Greenwillow Books."

Summary: It seems as though Trudy the goat knows when to expect snow,

but it turns out that she is really expecting something completely different.

ISBN 978-0-06-154267-1 (trade bdg.) — ISBN 978-0-06-154268-8 (lib. bdg.)

[1. Goats—Fiction. 2. Animals—Infancy—Fiction.] I. Title.

PZ7.C67345Tr 2009   [E]—dc22   2007047641

First Edition 10 9 8 7 6 5 4 3 2 1

Greenwillow Books

to my wonderful chums from long ago:
karen, joyce, betty kay, dody,
and . . . trudy!

also special thanks to justin c.,
for suggesting the idea of
a weather-predicting goat

It was Saturday that Esme's grandfather took her to the county auction. Lots of animals were for sale. Esme's grandfather had promised her one.

"*Moo-oo-oo*," bellowed a black-and-white cow,
nearly as tall as Grandfather.

"Oh! Can we get her, Grandfather?" asked Esme.

"Nope," answered Grandfather. "Got no room for a Holstein."

A large rooster in a cage puffed out its chest feathers.
"*Cccrrock-a-doodle-doo!*" it crowed.
"Oh! Can we get him?" Esme asked.
"Nope," Grandfather replied. "You know your
grandmother is allergic to feathers."

Esme peeked into a fenced pen. Inside were several enormous hogs.
Nope, she thought. *Too stinky!*

She considered an assortment of ducks.

And two guinea hens in a crate.

And a flock of pigeons.

Nope.
Nope.
And nope.

Then, from behind the legs of a pair of farmers, Esme noticed a single glittery eye. Over the eye hung a sign that read:

"TRUDY"

FREE

TO

GOOD HOME

Esme peeked over the
fence. There stood Trudy,
a brown and white goat.
"Oh!" said Esme. "Not too
big, not too small. Not too
stinky, and no feathers!"

Grandfather winked. "Well,"
he said, chuckling, "at least
the price is right!"

Trudy had found a home, or rather, a home had found Trudy:
a small red barn with a door that was just the right size for a goat.
Outside in the little yard, in a sunny corner underneath an apple
tree, there was a good spot for Trudy to sit.

Inside, Esme excitedly fluffed up clean straw and
made sure Trudy had fresh water and a bucket of food.

Esme scratched behind Trudy's ears as they sat
together in the straw. Sometimes she would read
stories aloud, or talk about her day at school.

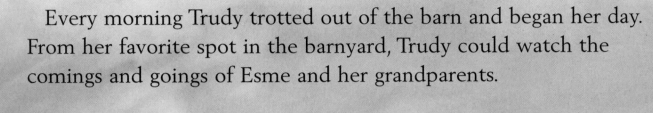

Every morning Trudy trotted out of the barn and began her day.
From her favorite spot in the barnyard, Trudy could watch the
comings and goings of Esme and her grandparents.

One cold, cloudy morning, Trudy stood in her favorite spot
under the apple tree. She sniffed the air. Her ears flicked in one direction,
then another. She sniffed again. Then she ambled back into the barn.

After school Esme stopped by with a treat for Trudy.
She was surprised to find Trudy inside the barn.
 "Trudy? You okay?" she asked.
 Esme stood outside the barn door and tried coaxing her out.
 "Trudy?" she called. But Trudy stayed inside, up to her chin in straw.
 Then it started to snow.

A beautiful blanket of snow fell, covering the
landscape from hillsides to apple tree twigs.

A week or so later, Esme noticed that Trudy was
again absent from her favorite corner in the barnyard.

"Looks like snow," Grandfather remarked.

"It looks like snow to Trudy, too," said Esme.
"She stays inside when the clouds say snow."

Sure enough, later that afternoon the flakes
started falling.

On the fourteenth, Trudy stayed inside.
On the fourteenth, it snowed.
On the twenty-seventh, Trudy stayed inside.
On the twenty-seventh, it snowed.

Grandmother said, "That goat is a natural-born weather forecaster!"

By the twenty-eighth, word had spread.

Mr. Nichols from next door came over. "Heard you've got quite a goat!" he said, laughing.

Miss Patterson stopped by. "What's the weather going to do today?" she hollered from her car. "Is it going to snow?"

More neighbors came over.

"Wonderin' if there'll be school tomorrow!"
"Maybe I can go cross-country skiing this weekend!"
Then again on the fifth, Trudy stayed inside.
Snow was predicted.
An inch fell before
midnight.

I GET MY WEATHER
REPORTS FROM
TRUDY

EZ PLZ

On Saturday a reporter came from the *Bluemont Mirror* and interviewed Esme. "She's quite a goat!" Esme exclaimed proudly.

On Sunday Channel 8 decided to set up cameras near Trudy's yard. "She may only be a goat, but she's got the inside scoop on the weather!" said a reporter.

"Look! She's heading inside!" shouted a woman wearing a pink sweatshirt with I GET MY WEATHER REPORTS FROM TRUDY on the front. Everyone watched as Trudy stepped quietly into the barn. Then all eyes searched the sky. Only a few wispy puffs dotted the blue.

"Must be an *evenin'* storm heading this way," said one man, as morning became afternoon.

"Or maybe just flurries today," remarked another.

Night came, but the snow did not.
The stars twinkled like sugar crystals.
People began to get bored.
"Hey! What gives?" grumbled one man.
"Humph!" snorted a woman, stomping off.
"Some prediction this turned out to be!"
And then, one by one, the crowd departed.
The reporters left. The cameramen gathered
up their gear and drove off. It was late.

"Oh, Trudy," Esme said. "I hope you're not sick."
She felt Trudy's forehead. She scratched behind
Trudy's ears. "If you're not perkier tomorrow, I'm
calling Dr. Roberts," she said, closing up for the night.
Trudy was left alone in her little red barn.

In the morning Esme jumped out of bed and hurried to the window.
The flagstone pathway below was clear of snow. Not one single snowflake
had fallen that night.

Now Esme was really worried. "Something's wrong with Trudy,
I just know it," she said to herself.

She quickly gathered up Trudy's favorite treats. She found an old, soft blanket. She even looked up Dr. Roberts's office number in the phone book.

Then she raced to the barn.

She quietly opened the barn door. Trudy was sitting peacefully in the straw, ears flicking.

And there, next to her, was a tiny, miniature version of Trudy. "Oh!" Esme whispered. "A baby!"

Trudy's baby stood on wobbly legs. "Beh-eh-eh-eh!" it bleated.
Esme watched as the kid shakily made its way to the door.
Trudy's baby looked outside.
  And then it began to rain; a warm, springtime rain. . . .